EGMONT

We bring stories to life

First published in Great Britain 2011 by Egmont UK Limited
239 Kensington High Street, London W8 6SA

Text copyright © Portobello Rights Limited 2011
Illustrations © Portobello Rights Limited and the BBC 2011,
taken from the BBC series 'World of Happy by Giles Andreae'
based on original illustrations by Janet Cronin

Giles Andreae has asserted his moral rights

A CIP catalogue record for this title is available from the British Library

ISBN 978 1 4052 5838 8
1 3 5 7 9 10 8 6 4 2
Printed in Italy

the little penguin

by giles andreae

original illustrations by janet cronin

a story about BEING BRAVE

my name is ....

and I did something really brave when

....

....

....

There was once a little penguin . . .

who was FRIGHTENED of the water.

"This is no way for PENGUINS to behave!" said his father.

"Be gentle," said his mother, "for ALL of us have fears that others may find hard to understand."

"Come, little penguin.
Come into the water with ME."

"But what if it's COLD?" said the penguin.

"What if there's a big fat scary monster?

And . . . what if I can't swim?"

"Ah," said his mother. "But what if it's LIGHT and BEAUTIFUL? What if all your brothers and sisters are there?"

"Come, little penguin, take my hand."

And with great COURAGE and great TRUST, the little penguin slipped into the water.

And for the first time in his life . . .

... he felt the JOY and freedom, WONDER and delight that EVERY penguin's heart is BORN to know.